The Queen & Mr Brown
A Day for Dinosaurs

James Francis Wilkins

Published by the Natural History Museum, London

For Lucie, Linus, Stella, Pia, Alexandros
and Her Majesty, with affection.
Especial thanks to Steve and Colin.

First published by the Natural History Museum
Cromwell Road, London SW7 5BD

Hardback edition

ISBN 978 0 565 09325 9
reprinted 2014

Paperback edition

ISBN 978 0 565 09354 9

A catalogue record for this book is available from the British Library.

Reproduction by Saxon Digital Services
Printed in China by C&C Offset Printing Co., Ltd

The Queen drew back the curtains and looked out.

"Mr Brown, it's snowing!" she called. He padded to the window and propped his paws against the sill. Flakes of wet snow were falling like stones from the sky. It was grey, gloomy and unbearably miserable.

Thank heavens he was inside in the warmth!

"They're like blobs of cotton wool. Aren't they beautiful", she continued. Mr Brown could see no beauty. He saw only a horrible, wet, cold day.

The Queen was not deterred. "I think we'll visit the dinosaurs today", she said.

After breakfast she dressed Mr Brown and put on her warmest coat. She would not let the weather spoil her day off. They would make the best of it and visit the dinosaurs at the Natural History Museum in South Kensington.

They went out through the side entrance of the Palace. Mr Brown shuddered. He hated snow, especially snow like this. This was certainly not weather for a royal corgi! But the Queen was insistent so he tucked his head into his coat and stepped out cautiously.

The weather was no obstacle to the tourists. A group of them stood gazing through the Palace railings. The Queen sometimes felt like a monkey in a cage. She half expected that they would try feeding her peanuts one day.

The Queen and Mr Brown joined the lines of people who were crossing the park. Some were on their way to work, others to shop. They kept their heads down

against the weather and said little. It was like a silent ballet. The Queen smiled at her little friend. “It’s a good day for dinosaurs, isn’t it.”

It took them half an hour to walk to the Museum, by which time Mr Brown was as miserable as the weather. He would have preferred to stay at home and watch television from a comfortable chair.

As they entered the Museum Mr Brown froze in his tracks. He had not been there before and had no idea what to expect. What he saw shocked him.

An immense dinosaur skeleton, stretching the length of the entrance hall, peered down at visitors as they came in. Mr Brown knew it was dead but he was taking no chances.

Even a dead dinosaur must be treated with extreme caution. He tried to make himself small and pressed close to the Queen.

They left their coats in the cloakroom and walked to the Dinosaur Gallery. More giant skeletons stood in rows. The Queen wondered what they had looked like when they were alive, for no-one has seen a living dinosaur.

They lived long long ago, before there were people on the Earth, and they were the most powerful of all creatures. But then, for some strange reason, they all died out.

There were many types of dinosaur. Some, like Brachiosaurus, Diplodocus and Manenchisaurus, were vegetarian. They had very long necks so that they could eat from trees.

Others, like Megalosaurus, Carnotaurus and Tyrannosaurus rex, were ferocious meat-eaters. They had large heads and strong back legs for running after their prey.

Once Mr Brown had grown used to the skeletons he was quickly bored and wandered off by himself. But the Queen was fascinated. She wanted to understand everything and read all that there was to read.

She looked in awe at the model of a Tyrannosaurus rex. It had teeth seven inches long in a mouth so big it could have swallowed her whole. It was so realistic it seemed to be alive.

She gazed in wonder at another display. It was the right foot of an Iguanodon which had suffered from arthritis one hundred million years ago, just like people do now. Nothing really changes, she thought.

And then she read how the dinosaurs had died out. Scientists think that a gigantic rock fell from the sky, stirring up so much dust that the sun was hidden for three months. This caused the Earth to become very, very cold. Too cold for dinosaurs.

This is probably what happened, but maybe... just maybe...

they killed themselves by jumping off a cliff...

they were overwhelmed by the stink of their own poo...

they bored themselves to death...

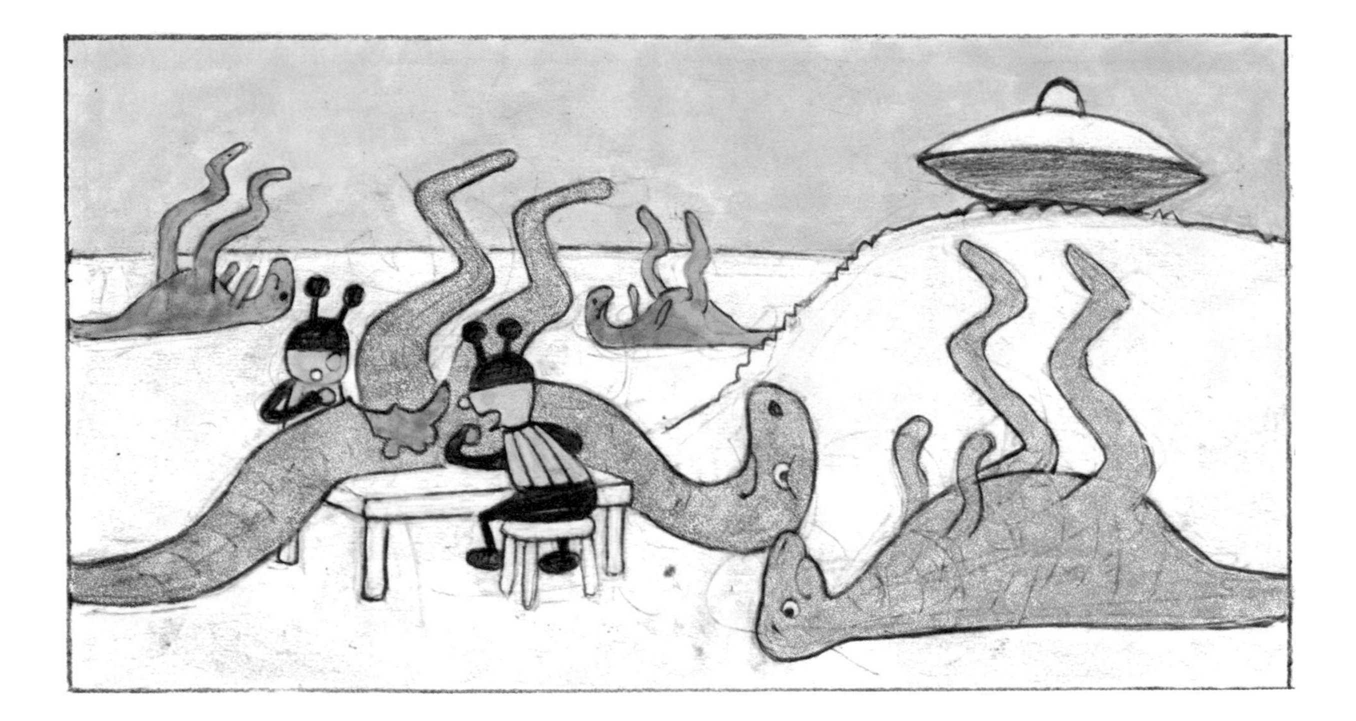

or aliens came from outer space and ate them for breakfast.

As the Queen stood imagining the various possibilities, it occurred to her that she hadn't seen Mr Brown for a long time. She hurried off to search for him and found him fast asleep, stretched out in front of a huge bone.

He woke up and they looked at it together.

"Left thigh-bone of an Apatosaurus", she read. It was as tall as she was. Not even in his dreams had Mr Brown imagined such a magnificent bone.

They had now spent half the day in the Museum and the Queen was beginning to feel tired. She sat down on a bench and ate a sandwich. She then fed Mr Brown some biscuits while she thought about all the things they had seen.

It was pleasantly warm in the Museum and it wasn't long before she found herself nodding off to sleep. Mr Brown flopped down next to her and closed his eyes.

In the distance she could hear a noise, a familiar noise, and one she loved to hear.

It was the sound of the crowd at Ascot, and they were chanting a name, over and over again. As she listened she suddenly realised that it was her name they were chanting. She was not watching a race, she was taking part in one!

Her mount was lunging forward with giant strides. Instinctively she urged it on, but it was such a powerful beast she had difficulty controlling it.

She had an even bigger shock when she glanced down. It was not a horse she was riding...

...it was a Megalosaurus! The giant creature was pounding along, snorting out breath. And with every footfall the ground shuddered and

she was jolted violently and nearly thrown from its back. The Queen was a good rider but she had never ridden a monster like this!

The crowd were chanting her name because she
was leading the race! But she hardly heard them as
she needed all her concentration to avoid being

thrown under the feet of the other dinosaurs. They raced around the final curve of the track and thundered down the home straight.

The finishing post was in sight and she dug her feet into the animal's side, spurring it on. She only had to keep going to be the winner and she liked winning!

But the crowd had started to chant another name and she could hear another dinosaur close behind her and getting closer. She glanced over her shoulder only to see...

...the tiny body of Mr Brown bouncing up and down like a ball on the back of a Carnotaurus. It was his name that the crowd was chanting now.

He was just as determined to win as the Queen was and he held on doggedly until he was almost level with her.

As they came up to the winning post, Mr Brown's dinosaur dipped its head like a sprinter and crossed the line inches ahead of the Queen's dinosaur.

The Queen could hardly believe it. She had been pipped at the post by her best friend. It was just too annoying!

The crowd surged excitedly around Mr Brown and his Carnotaurus as it was led into the winner's enclosure, sweating and steaming. Everybody clapped and cheered and Mr Brown was ecstatic.

He sprang from his mount in a victory leap as he had seen it done on television, for he had spent many afternoons watching horse racing and knew all about it.

But what he did not know, until this moment, was the beautiful feeling of winning.

He was presented with the winner's trophy which had his name engraved on it, under those of the previous winners.

His joy was boundless and his stumpy little tail just wouldn't stop wagging.

“Madam, we’re closing now”, said a friendly voice. The Queen tried to focus her thoughts and looked up to see a Museum attendant smiling down at her.

“Dear me, I must have been sleeping”, she said as she got to her feet.

"I'll show you to the exit", he said and walked along beside them. "I don't blame you for coming in here in this weather", he continued, "I hope you've got a nice, warm home to go back to?"

"Thank you, yes yes, I do. That's very kind of you to enquire", she replied, quite touched by his concern.

The weather outside was now truly atrocious, with driving snow. Mr Brown struggled through the slush and icy puddles. His stubby little legs were not designed for this.

The Queen remained strangely silent. For some funny reason, perhaps wounded pride, she did not feel like telling him about her dream.

But eventually she did say something. “I wonder why the dinosaurs really did die out?”

Mr Brown grimaced. Sometimes he just did not understand her. If he had been able to speak he would have screamed out “IT’S BECAUSE THEY WENT OUT IN WEATHER LIKE THIS!”

But he kept quiet and thought of his warm basket waiting for him back at the Palace.